Dear Parent:
Your child's love of reading starts here!

Every child learns to read in a different way and at his or her own speed. You can help your young reader improve and become more confident by encouraging his or her own interests and abilities. You can also guide your child's spiritual development by reading stories with biblical values and Bible stories, like I Can Read! books published by Zonderkidz. From books your child reads with you to the first books he or she reads alone, there are I Can Read! books for every stage of reading:

SHARED READING
Basic language, word repetition, and whimsical illustrations, ideal for sharing with your emergent reader.

BEGINNING READING
Short sentences, familiar words, and simple concepts for children eager to read on their own.

READING WITH HELP
Engaging stories, longer sentences, and language play for developing readers.

READING ALONE
Complex plots, challenging vocabulary, and high-interest topics for the independent reader.

ADVANCED READING
Short paragraphs, chapters, and exciting themes for the perfect bridge to chapter books.

I Can Read! books have introduced children to the joy of reading since 1957. Featuring award-winning authors and illustrators and a fabulous cast of beloved characters, I Can Read! books set the standard for beginning readers.

A lifetime of discovery begins with the magical words "I Can Read!"

Visit www.icanread.com for information on enriching your child's reading experience.
Visit www.zonderkidz.com for more Zonderkidz I Can Read! titles.

"Although they cannot repay you, you will be
repaid at the resurrection of the righteous."
—*Luke 14:14b*

ZONDERKIDZ

Princess Joy's Party
Copyright © 2012 by Zonderkidz

Requests for information should be addressed to:

Zonderkidz, 5300 Patterson Ave. SE, Grand Rapids, Michigan 49530

Library of Congress Control Number: 2012932644

Editor: Mary Hassinger
Art direction & design: Diane Mielke

Printed in China

14 15 16 17 /DSC/ 7 6 5 4

ZONDERkidz

I Can Read!™

BEGINNING 1 READING

The Princess Parables™

Princess Joy's Party

Story inspired by **Jeanna Young** & **Jacqueline Johnson**

Pictures by **Omar Aranda**

Princess Joy lives in a castle.

She has four sisters.

They are Grace, Faith, Charity, and Hope.

Their daddy is the king!

It was time for Joy to wake up.

"Woof!" barked Rosebud.

Princess Joy said, "Good morning, Rosebud."

Princess Joy walked to the window.

Joy's sisters were in the garden below.

Princess Hope said,

"Joy will be surprised!"

Grace said, "Yes, Joy loves birthdays.

A surprise party is a good idea."

"Shh," said Hope. "Not too loud.

Joy might hear us."

Princess Joy was so happy!

She danced with Rosebud.

"A surprise party just for me?"

God had blessed Joy with kind

and caring sisters indeed.

Faith, Grace, Charity, and Hope

sent invitations.

They asked all of Princess Joy's

friends to come to the party.

But there was bad news!

"Oh, no," said Princess Charity.

"Another friend cannot come

to Joy's birthday party.

What will we do?"

Joy soon heard the bad news.

No one could come to her party.

Princess Joy was very sad.

"I do not want a party.

I do not want a birthday at all!"

said Joy.

Later that day,

Joy saw her sisters and daddy playing

and having fun.

Some of her sadness went away.

Being with her family made Joy

happy.

Then Princess Joy had a great idea!

Joy wanted other people

to be this happy too.

Joy said, "Daddy, I have a big idea."

Princess Joy said, "Daddy, I DO want a birthday party.

Let's invite boys and girls from the village.

Some of them do not have big families or big, fancy parties.

I want them to feel happy just like we are!"

The king said, "God gave you a good heart. God bless you, Joy."

And this time,

all the boys and girls said yes!

The sisters baked cakes.

They made pretty decorations.

The princesses picked flowers too. Joy, Faith, Grace, Hope, and Charity all helped get ready for Joy's party.

The day of the party came.

All of the boys and girls were at the

castle on time.

They even brought special gifts for Joy!

Joy said, "Thank you for coming
to my birthday party.
I am glad you are all here!"

Joy's birthday party was fun.

The princesses made new friends.

All of the children were happy.

They sang songs, drank punch,

and ate delicious cake.

Joy was blessed with family, new

friends, and God's love.

Then it was time for gifts from Joy's family!

The princesses helped to carry many gifts to the party.

There were so many presents for Joy.

Joy went to talk to her father.

She said, "I have so many things.

May I share my gifts

with my new friends?"

The king thought about Joy's idea.

He knew it was a good idea.

"Yes, Joy," said the king.

"You can share your gifts
with your new friends."

So Princess Joy sat

on the king's throne.

Charity, Hope, Faith, and Grace

were with her.

Then the king made a short speech.

The king said, "Children,

thank you for coming to Joy's party.

You have helped make her very happy.

Now Joy wants to share

her happiness with you!"

After all the happy children went home,

Joy prayed, "Dear God,

thank you for the best birthday ever.

And thank you for my new friends.

I wanted to show them my love,

but now, I feel more loved than ever.

Thank you for this great gift

of love!"